Poor Little Egg-Boy Hatched in a Shul

NATHAN ENGLANDER

Illustrations by Jordin Isip

MERYL GELERNTER was peeling eggs at the kitchen sink of the Hempelbrew Synagogue when she peeled an egg that was her son. She pulled off the shell to reveal a face sticking out from the white, two arms sticking out from the sides, and two legs poking out from the place where legs go.

She turned off the water and set the boy down on the floor.

On the floor, Meryl's son was suddenly kid-sized—kid-sized but a perfect egg-boy. Meryl thought, in admiring her son and then admiring his white, that this would be a perfect hard-boiled-egg costume—just the way you'd want to make it, if it weren't in fact real. Perfect, except for the part of the white that was torn. She'd have been more careful in cracking the shell and peeling it back if she'd known her son was inside.

As for the very noticeable, very exponential change from egg-sized boy to boy-sized egg, she'd have thought it strange if not for what preceded it—if she hadn't just peeled an egg that was her son. And, of course, there'd been

4

sacre bleu!!!

a rash of such happenings in Hempelbrew of late. There was peach-girl and banana-boy and a lobster, not really human, though it screamed, upon boiling, in French.

Meryl crossed her arms and said, "An egg-boy. Well, I'll be!" Then she locked up the synagogue and took her son home.

Now, Meryl hadn't planned for this. She had an urgent errand to run. But, egg or no, a mother cannot leave a little boy unattended. It's irresponsible. Which is why Meryl Gelernter fetched her other child—her older child—from the neighbors' across the way.

Meryl left her egg-son in her daughter's care. All she said to her daughter was, "Watch him." Then she turned back and added, "Don't eat him!"

The problem for the egg-boy was this: like many little boys, he really loved egg whites. He had no feeling for yolks. But the white… there was nothing better.

While he was waiting with his sister, he just couldn't resist. It looked so tasty, and he was already torn. He reached up and, taking hold of the broken part, pulled off a perfect strip. Like an egg-slicer slice. A single round.

And he ate it. The egg-boy ate himself— which he kind of felt, even in the moment, must be wrong.

When his mother returned and saw

eats self

the missing strip, she was very mad at her daughter for eating her son. She'd expressly told her not to.

The daughter protested her innocence, but her mother wouldn't hear it. What kind of little boy would eat himself? she wanted to know.

"Little brothers," the daughter said, "do worse."

The egg-boy didn't say a word.

He said nothing then, and went on saying nothing even when his father got home. It was to his father that the egg-boy's mother declared, "Look what she's done, she's half eaten our son. We can't trust our daughter anymore."

The egg-boy's father thought she should

sleep in the basement behind a locked door. His mother said no. His father thought they could, maybe just for that evening, keep her in their closet and nail the whole thing shut. Again Meryl said no. It was not safe to have a daughter who doesn't listen under the same roof as their son.

Meryl Gelernter took her daughter across the street and gave her to the neighbors to raise.

Our poor little egg-boy did not open his mouth at dinner that night, for fear the truth would escape. He said nothing at breakfast the next morning, when his father let out a terrible sigh.

The egg-boy soldiered on that way for a

can't sleep

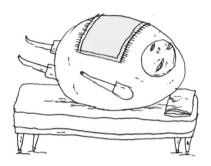

number of days, always telling himself that
not-saying was different than lying.

When his closed-mouthed hunger became
too great, and his sister-based guilt too strong,
when finally the egg-boy wanted to set the
record straight, he assembled his family (waving

13

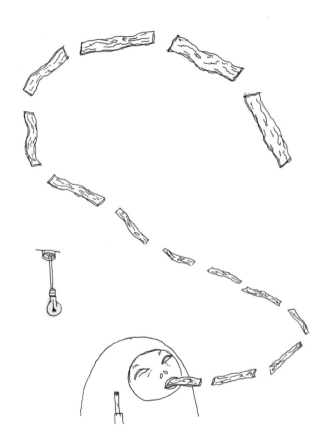

his sister over to the window), ready to tell them the truth.

The egg-boy was proud to be doing what was right.

But *what's* right and *when* it's right can be two different things.

The egg-boy opened his mouth and discovered he'd waited too long. Ready to talk, there were no words left.

His tongue had turned to bacon.

Nathan Englander is the author of *The Ministry of Special Cases*, a novel, and the short story collection *For the Relief of Unbearable Urges*. He lives in New York City.

Virgil Walker

ARTHUR BRADFORD

Illustrations by Jon Adams

IMAGINE MRS. WALKER'S surprise upon giving birth to a squirming octopus instead of the little human baby she had been expecting.

"I'm afraid I don't know how to care for an octopus," she said. So she placed him carefully in a bucket of salt water and left him on the stoop of a local pet shop with a note.

His name is Virgil, it said.

❧

THE OWNER of the pet shop was a round man named Mr. Lopez. Mr. Lopez's shop had rows and rows of tanks with dozens of colored fish inside of them. When the shop was open, customers would walk by and tap on Virgil's tank and smile at him. Virgil tried to smile back and wave his arms about in a friendly way, but nobody wanted an octopus for a pet. They all wanted pretty fish.

Some of the colored fish residing in the tank across from Virgil saw his attempts to impress the customers and laughed at him, as small fish are wont to do.

"Hee, hee, hee!" they tittered.

So that night, after the shop closed, Virgil crawled out of his tank, across the floor, and ate six of the fish. And then he returned to his tank, his belly full.

❧

THE NEXT MORNING, Mr. Lopez noticed that some of his fish were gone. He looked everywhere for them, but their disappearance was a mystery.

"What happened to my fish?" he bellowed.

He checked the locks on his doors and windows, but saw no signs of forced entry.

"Hmmm…" he said to himself.

That night, Virgil crept out of his tank once again. He ate more fish. He did this for several nights in a row, until nearly all of the shop's fish were gone.

The pet shop owner was beside himself. "My fish are disappearing!" he cried. In an effort to solve the mystery, he installed a video camera to record what happened while he was away.

❧

ONCE AGAIN, Virgil crept out at night, and this time he ate the remaining fish. He was about to crawl back into his tank when he heard a dignified voice call out to him.

"Excuse me, my good man," said a wrinkled old turtle. "Would you be so kind as to release me from this tank?"

Virgil said, "I'd be glad to," and with his long arm he tipped the turtle's tank on its side.

"Why thank you," said the turtle. He slowly walked over to the doorway of the pet shop, and with one click of his powerful jaw he snapped the lock.

"Let's go," said the turtle.

"Okay," said Virgil. And together they set off into the night.

As they strolled the streets together, Virgil observed that he and the turtle looked somewhat different than everyone else.

"What we need," said Virgil, "are some nice clothes."

"I wholeheartedly concur," said the turtle, whose name was Mr. Beeker.

They found a late-night gentleman's shop and convinced the shopkeeper to sell them formal suits on credit.

"We will gladly pay you the balance due at a future date," said Mr. Beeker. "With interest, of course."

In truth, the shopkeeper was glad to be rid of his octopus and turtle suits. They had not been selling well.

"Where shall we go now?" said Virgil, who looked spiffy indeed in his new houndstooth attire.

"I suppose we should go dancing," said Mr. Beeker, who had been cooped up in his tank at the pet store for well over a year.

So they went to the Rainbow Room, where gentlemen and ladies were known to dance to the big-band sounds.

Despite their fine new outfits, the doorman at the Rainbow Room was reluctant at first to admit Mr. Beeker and Virgil, but it wasn't long before two sleek ladies took them by the arms and whisked them inside.

"I want to dance with you!" said one lady to Virgil, and together they hit the dance floor.

Boy could that Virgil dance! He wiggled about

the dance floor like electrified jelly. Mr. Beeker
and his date simply watched from the bar while
sipping brandy. It was a long and enjoyable night.

THE NEXT MORNING Mr. Lopez returned to his
shop and found it quite empty. All of the animals
were gone. He examined the tapes from the
camera he had installed and saw that it was Virgil

and Mr. Beeker who had caused the trouble. He filed a report with the police, and the next morning Virgil and Mr. Beeker's faces appeared in the newspaper under the headline WANTED: FOR GRAND THEFT.

Virgil and Mr. Beeker were enjoying a leisurely breakfast at an outdoor café with their two lady friends when they were apprehended by the police. Virgil and Mr. Beeker were shipped off

to Rikers Island jail, where they awaited trial for nearly nine months. Finally their day in court arrived.

At their trial, Mr. Lopez showed the videotape of Virgil escaping from his tank, eating the fish, releasing Mr. Beeker, and then walking out the door. The jury shook their heads. Things did not look good for the two animals. But then, when it came time for their defense, Mr. Beeker stood up and addressed the court himself.

Old Mr. Beeker was very eloquent, having been trained in law years ago by a scholarly tortoise. He made the case that Virgil was not responsible for his actions.

"He's a victim of society!" shouted Mr. Beeker. "His mother abandoned him in a bucket on the steps of Mr. Lopez's shop! I ask you, ladies and gentlemen of the jury, would you have acted any differently if placed in poor Virgil's predicament?"

Some members of the jury were seen welling up with tears.

And then, for his pièce de résistance, Mr. Beeker called a character witness to the stand. In walked Virgil's date from the Rainbow Room, the stylish woman with whom he'd spent the night. She was pregnant, nearly bursting with child, and the entire courtroom gasped when she testified:

"This child belongs to Virgil."

Mr. Beeker went on to tug at the heartstrings of the jury, and they were both acquitted on the grounds that society owed them this mercy. On the steps of the courtroom Virgil made a short statement:

"I'd like to thank you all."

And then he left with his pregnant companion to attend to their affairs.

⚓

VIRGIL'S CHILD was born shortly afterward, a son, and for the most part he resembled a human boy, except for a small tail sprouting from his backside and tiny suction cups dimpling his palms. The boy's mother was a little distressed, and told Virgil she wasn't sure how to raise such a child.

"I shall attend to him," said Virgil.

And with that he took his newborn son down to the waterfront and placed him in a small, floatable box. He fashioned a sail out of cloth and attached it to the vessel so as to give it speed. Then he set his son afloat and watched him drift away, out into the sea, where he hoped some fellow octopuses might take notice. On the side of the box Virgil had written a note.

His name is Virgil, it said.

Arthur Bradford lives in Portland, Oregon, and is the director of the TV series *How's Your News?* on MTV (howsyournews.com). His first book, *Dogwalker*, was published by Knopf in 2001, and is out in Vintage paperback now. In the summertime, he directs Camp Jabberwocky, the oldest sleepaway camp for people with disabilities in the United States.

The Book and the Girl

BRIAN EVENSON

Illustrations by Phillip Fivel Nessen

ONCE THERE WAS A BOOK who loved a little

girl. The little girl would spend her days with

the book. She stood on him when she needed

something off the counter. She wore him as a

hat. When she was tired she used him for a

pillow. Best of all, she read him. She read him

to her hamster, to her dog, to the wall. The book

liked to hear himself speaking in her voice. The

girl loved him very much, and he was happy.

But time went by. And the girl grew older. And the world changed. The sky grew dark, and rain came that wouldn't stop. Everything went wrong with the world. The girl worried and worried. And the book was often alone.

And then one day a light came that was so bright you could see your own bones. The girl had to leave very quickly. The book watched her get ready, begging her silently not to forget him.

And, at the last moment, she didn't.

The girl walked for many miles. Each night, when she stopped, she would take the book out and wonder why she had brought him. Sometimes people laughed at her for bringing a book. "Throw it away," they said. But she

couldn't bring herself to leave her book behind.

Soon she had holes in the bottoms of her shoes. That night she took the book out and said, "Why didn't I pack a second pair of shoes instead of you, book?"

But you did, the book wanted to say. But he couldn't speak. All he could do was will the girl to look closer.

And she did. She cut new soles out of the book's leather cover, and they were better than the soles she'd first had. The girl was glad she had kept the book.

And the book, though there was less of him, was happy.

Soon the girl became hungry. That night

she took the book out and said, "Why didn't I pack more food instead of you, book?"

But you did, the book wanted to say. But he couldn't speak. All he could do was will the girl to look closer.

And she did. She tore off the rest of his cover and boiled it with herbs to make a soup, and though it wasn't the best meal, it was enough to keep her alive. The girl was glad she had brought the book.

And the book, though there was even less of him, was happy.

Soon it became very cold. That night the girl took the book out and said, "Why didn't I pack another blanket instead of you, book?"

But you did, the book wanted to say. But he couldn't speak. All he could do was will the girl to look closer.

And she did. She snapped the threads binding his pages together until she had a pile of loose paper. She crumpled these and stuffed them into her clothes, where they kept her warm and dry. The girl was glad she had brought the book.

And the book, though in pieces now, was happy.

❧

AFTER MANY DAYS, the girl came to a new place. She knocked on a door until it opened for her. It was warm inside, and there was food and a bed.

Then she remembered the book. She fished its crumpled pages from her clothes. She smoothed them out and arranged them as best she could. And then, haltingly, she began to read aloud.

At first, the book, though battered, was pleased to hear himself speaking through the girl's voice. *People must be pleased to hear us,* the girl thought. But when she looked up, she saw everyone staring out the windows. A great, withering darkness roiled toward them across the plains. They watched in silence, waiting.

The girl turned back to the book and tried to keep reading. But soon it was clear that there were too many smudged words, too many missing pages. The book didn't know what he was saying, his story was no longer a story, and all of it was powerless against what was coming for them next.

Brian Evenson is the author of eight books of fiction, most recently *The Open Curtain*, which was a finalist for an Edgar Award. A new collection of his short fiction, *Fugue State*, will be published by Coffee House Press next year. He lives in Providence, Rhode Island, where he directs Brown University's Literary Arts Program.

This story, a portion of McSweeney's 28, is © 2008 Brian Evenson and Phillip Fivel Nessen. Back cover painting by Danica Novgorodoff.

The Box

SARAH MANGUSO

Illustrations by Louie Cordero

A MAN keeps a locked box in the attic.

He is an uncomplicated man. He works and looks after himself.

A lady comes to see him. She kisses his face and neck. *What's in the box?* she asks him. *It's nothing*, he says.

After the man falls asleep, the lady climbs to the attic. She removes a hairpin to pick the lock, but there isn't time. The man is calling to her.

The lady's friends ask her about the man. He keeps a box of jewels in the attic, she tells them.

The man's neighbor hears of a box of money and stops him on the street. *Tell me what you have in there*, he says. *It's just a box*, the man says.

The neighbor comes at night to open it. He has brought a file, a hammer, an axe, and dynamite. He is an inexperienced burglar. He drops his hammer. Now he has made too much noise and must leave by the window.

The man's mother hears of a box full of secrets. She asks her son to open the box.

The man brings his mother to the attic. He shakes the box; it makes a hollow sound. *The box is empty*, he says. She squints at him. *Where have you put the family secrets? I am your mother*, she says. The man says, *Secrets? This box is an empty box*. The man's mother tells her friends of her unkind son.

Now the box has caused some excitement, and the man finds himself liking the attention. *What is in the box?* People ask on the street and on the phone. *I can't tell you*, he says, feeling slippery and strong. Hundreds of people ask, cajole, trick. The man resists in a hundred ways.

People begin to find him fascinating. They believe he is powerful and brilliant. He is given a promotion at work. Shortly afterward, he is elected mayor.

People no longer remember a time when they didn't adore him. They create a new position between mayor and king, which they call *ming*. He is named ming.

He is given a palace and a throne. Next to his throne, on a table of solid gold, the box is placed. All this time, it has not been opened. The man does not want it opened, for he believes that its mystery holds its power—and his power.

But the people no longer care what's in the
box. They only care that the man denied them.
They love him because he said no.

Sarah Manguso is the author of four books, most recently the memoir *The Two Kinds of Decay* (Farrar, Straus and Giroux, 2008) and the collection *Hard to Admit and Harder to Escape*, which appeared in *One Hundred and Forty-Five Stories in a Small Box* (McSweeney's, 2007).

The Guy Who Kept Meeting Himself

RYAN BOUDINOT

Illustrations by Genevieve Simms

PETER STARTED MEETING older versions
of himself when he was six years old. He
was sitting on a bench in front of the library,
waiting for his mother to pick him up, when
a twelve-year-old sat beside him. The boy
looked like he could have been Peter's older
brother, but in fact it was Peter himself, years
later. He wore a cool jean jacket and his hair
was styled in a mullet.

"What's up?" older Peter said.

"I got a book about spiders," younger Peter said.

And that was about the extent of the conversation, because younger Peter's mom arrived. She didn't notice the older, shaggier version of her own son.

A few years passed and Peter was fifteen, hanging out in a food court, drinking a blackberry milk shake. A twenty-five-year-old version of himself sat down. Young Peter thought about the first time he'd met an older version of himself and how he had blown the chance to ask him questions about the future. This time he was prepared.

"When do I lose my virginity?" young Peter said.

"You sure you wanna know?"

"Yeah."

"Third year of college, October 12, 1991."

Young Peter was so disappointed with the answer he forgot to ask any other questions.

Sure enough, when October 12, 1991 rolled around, Peter finally convinced a girl to sleep with him. They ended up getting married after graduation and having two kids in quick succession. Peter put his electrical engineering degree to work as a computer programmer. It was hard work, but he made a lot of money in the tech boom. Still, he suspected that true happiness eluded him. By the time another future self paid him a visit, he had a six-bedroom house and three cars. The future self was forty-one. He walked up to Peter one morning while younger Peter was stretching for his daily jog. They looked fairly similar, though older Peter had less hair and a thicker middle.

"Spend more time with your kids," older Peter said.

"Easy for you to say," younger Peter said, then asked his older self for any hot stock tips.

"You sure you want to know?" the older man said.

"Of course I'm sure."

The older self obliged, naming some companies

that didn't exist yet. In the coming years Peter
would make out big with his investments.
He'd buy a vacation house in Hawaii, which
was where he sat one afternoon at age forty-five,
enjoying the sunset, when a sixty-two-year-old
man appeared who was unmistakably himself.

"Hey, it's you again," said younger Peter.
"Say, my wife just found a lump in her breast.
Is she going to be all right?"

"You really want to know?"

"Yeah."

"The lump is irrelevant," older Peter said.
"Your wife is going to die in a car accident
next year, and there's nothing you can do to
prevent it."

"Thanks. Way to make my day," younger Peter said. In the following year—the worst year of his life so far—he did everything he could to prevent his wife from riding in cars. One night, just before Christmas, he let his guard down. She was in a car with her sister when they were hit by a drunk driver, and Peter's wife died instantly.

The kids went to college and Peter retired, living more or less permanently in his vacation home on the beach. Even though he'd become a very wealthy man, he regretted never living in the moment, and had come to hate his future selves for ruining all his surprises—good and bad. So when, at the age of sixty-seven, he met

his eighty-year-old self, he was prepared.

"When am I going to die?" he asked his older self, slowly reaching for the revolver hidden under a towel.

"You sure you really want to know?"

"Yes, yes I do."

"Right about now," the older Peter said sadly, stabbing the younger Peter in the chest with a knife he'd been hiding in his dungarees.

As younger Peter died, he looked up at his older self and whispered, "But *I* was going to kill *you*."

The older Peter shook his head. "Wasn't supposed to happen that way. I could have told you that."

Ryan Boudinot is the author of *The Littlest Hitler*.
He is on the faculty of Goddard College's MFA
program, in Port Townsend, Washington.

This story, a portion of McSweeney's 28, is © 2008 Ryan Boudinot
and Genevieve Simms. Back cover painting by Danica Novgorodoff.

Two Free Men

SHEILA HETI

Illustrations by Liz Lee

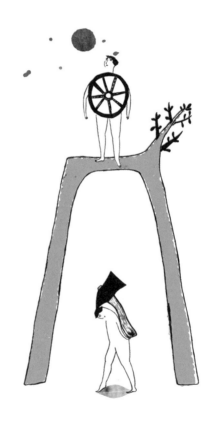

A DEPRESSED MAN and a suicidal man were hanging out near a tall wooden bridge over a muddy ravine. The depressed man was pacing below it, looking down—for depressed people never look up, only down. And the suicidal man was standing on the bridge's edge, talking himself into jumping.

Although one was above and the other was below, they had similar problems and similar reasons for being there. Both were living in a very strange country where every man's first obligation was to be "free." What this meant was: any time they felt themselves falling in love, they had to remind themselves that the proper thing to do was pull back. After all, a better girl might come along—and if they missed that opportunity, it would be like missing life itself.

Their lives in their city were provisional. After all, work opportunities might arise in other cities, meaning they'd have to move. So although they had apartments and friends,

they were only half-there in their homes, and half-there among their friends. The other half was ever on edge, in case something should call them away.

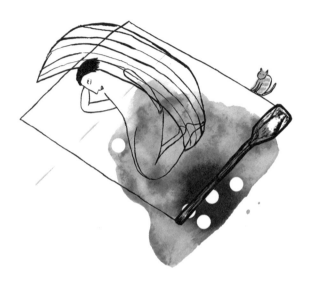

All of which, if you look at it, is a very lonely
way of being.

And they *were* lonely. One was suicidal, and
the other was depressed.

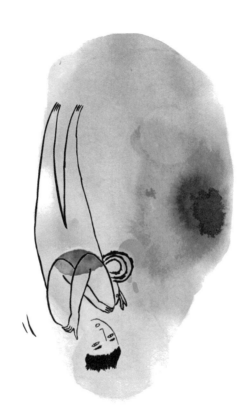

Well—and these things don't only happen
in stories!—the suicidal man stepped off the
bridge and fell through the air with increas-
ing speed, and expanding in his mind was the
thought, "I don't want to die!"—when he col-
lided in an awkward way with the depressed
man who was pacing below, collapsing them
both to the ground.

For a few minutes the men lay there groaning, rubbing their heads and elbows and knees, but once the shock began to subside, they raised themselves to look at each other. Two sets of brown eyes adjusted focus, then blinked. Each man was surprised to see how

similar he was to the other—in coloring, in physique, in expression. It was like meeting one's own double. The suicidal man was particularly shocked: his plan had been to end one life—and now he was confronted with two.

A feeling surfaced inside the depressed man like a rubber duck thrown in a tub: "I did something in this life! I saved a man from dying!" Then a thought came to him, which he couldn't help or prevent. He said to the suicidal man, speaking more seriously than he ever had before: "Don't worry. I will always be close by your side. I will always catch you when you fall."

Now, the suicidal man ought to have been repelled. No one, not even a woman, had ever promised to be by his side forever. But he was not put off at all. He felt something bloom in his heart, and a smile rise up to his face. He couldn't help it.

He replied, with a feeling of purpose growing inside him: "And I will keep jumping and falling."

Sheila Heti lives in Toronto. She is the author of the story collection, *The Middle Stories*, and the novel, *Ticknor*.

LaKeisha and the
Dirty Girl

TAYARI JONES

Illustrations by Morgan Elliott

LaKEISHA SHAUNTELLE ANDERSON was
a very lovely girl who owned everything her
heart desired, and hers was a heart with quite
an appetite. She was especially fond of books,
their straight edges and clean-paper scent. Her
greatest passion was for the dust jackets, for
their endless variety of colors and textures.

LaKeisha identified her books only by number,
having no curiosity about their titles or plots.
Every Wednesday, she touched her finger to the

beautiful spines, making sure each gorgeous text was in its place. On the third Wednesday in April, she discovered that book number 777 was missing. Oh where could it be?

The Sunday before, LaKeisha had taken 777 to the green-grassy park. Its cover, party-dress purple, matched her beaded sandals, and the gold-edged pages complemented her tinkly charm bracelet. She could not recall seeing it since that warm-park afternoon.

❧

A MONTH LATER, at the green-grassy park, LaKeisha spotted a dirty little girl leafing through a purple book with gold-edged pages.

The dirty girl's dress was too small for her, and the soles of her shoes flapped open as if they were trying to talk. This kind of girl didn't own books at all, no matter what her shoes were trying to say.

LaKeisha ran until she found a policeman sitting near the fountain, slurping soda pop and cleaning his ears with his keys.

"I want to report a theft!" LaKeisha said, tugging him to the park bench where the dirty girl was enjoying the pretty book so much that she didn't look up until the policeman snatched the book away.

"My book!" cried the dirty girl.

"*My* book!" said LaKeisha. "I count my books

every week. The number is written under the dust jacket."

"I didn't steal anything," the little girl said.

The policeman reached after her and only caught the pocket of her worn dress, ripping it away.

"You have torn my only dress," the little girl whimpered. "And you are taking my favorite book!"

"Stealing it doesn't make it yours," LaKeisha said.

"I found that book," sobbed the little girl. "I found it in the trash."

"She's a thief and a liar," LaKeisha said. "You don't find books like this in the trash."

The policeman pulled the dirty little girl by the arm, stepping on the ripped-away pocket as he dragged her toward the street.

❧

AFTER THEY HAD GONE, LaKeisha sat on the bench admiring the handsome book. The dirty girl had seemed quite interested in its contents, so LaKeisha thought maybe she would try reading the book herself. She stared at the endless rows of black print against plain white paper and quickly shut it, preferring instead to gaze at the sumptuous cover. On a whim, she peeked underneath.

And then she let out a little gasp and

jumped down from the bench.

Near the fountain was the policeman, busy
again with his ears.

"There's been a mistake!" LaKeisha said.
"This is not 777. Look here—there is no
number on it at all. That other little girl
didn't steal this from me."

"Doesn't matter," he said. "If she didn't steal
it from you, she stole it from someone."

"How do you know that?"

"How come you thought she stole it in the
first place?"

"Because she was dirty," LaKeisha whispered.

"I rest my case," said the officer. "Now run
along."

When LaKeisha returned to the bench, she found a small plastic bag. She untied the handles to see what other things the dirty girl owned. Inside was a cast-off sandwich, a brown apple core, and a dented yellow yo-yo that LaKeisha had thrown away just two days before. Underneath the bench, she noticed a small package wrapped in paper and tied with string. Unwrapping it, she discovered a jewel of a paperback, the same creamy peach as apricot sorbet.

LaKeisha swooned, pressing her lips to the shiny cover. "Oh my," she panted, kissing it again. "This is a truly remarkable book. I think I have just the hat to match it!"

Tayari Jones is the author of *Leaving Atlanta* and *The Untelling*. She teaches as part of the MFA faculty at Rutgers-Newark University.

This story, a portion of McSweeney's 28, is © 2008 Tayari Jones and Morgan Elliott. Back cover painting by Danica Novgorodoff.

The Thousands

DANIEL ALARCÓN

Illustrations by Jordan Awan

THERE WAS NO MOON that first night, and we spent it as we spent our days: your fathers and your mothers have always worked with their hands. We came in trucks and cleared the land of rock and debris, working in the pale yellow glow of the headlights, deciding by touch and smell and taste that the land was

good. We would raise our children here. Make
a life here. Understand that, not so long ago,
this was nowhere. This land had no owner, and
it had not yet been named. That first night, the
darkness that surrounded us seemed infinite,

and it would be false to say we were not afraid.
Some had tried this before and failed—in
other districts, on other fallow land. Some
of us sang to stay awake. Others prayed for
strength. It was a race, and we all knew it. The
law was very clear: while these sorts of things

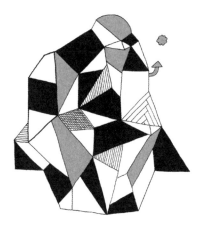

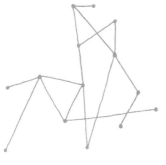

were not technically legal, the government was not allowed to bulldoze homes.

We had until morning to build them.

The hours passed, and by dawn the progress was undeniable. With a little imagination one could see the bare outlines of the place this would become. There were tents made of tarps and sticks. There were mats of woven reeds topped with sewn-together rice sacks, and sheets of pressboard leaning against the scavenged hoods of old cars. Everything the city discarded, we'd been saving for months in preparation for this first night. And now we worked and we worked, and for good measure, we spent the last hours of that long night

drawing roads on the earth, just lines of chalk
then, but think of it, just think... We could
see them, the avenues they would be, even if
no one else could. By morning it was all there,
this ramshackle collection of odds and ends,
and we couldn't help but feel pride.

When we finally stopped to rest, we realized we were cold, and on the soft slope of the hill dozens of small fires were built. We warmed ourselves, each taking comfort in it, in our numbers, in this land we had chosen. The day dawned with its pale golden light, the sky scoured clean and cloudless. It's pretty, we said, and the mountains were indeed beautiful that morning.

They still are. The government arrived before noon, and didn't know what to do. The bulldozers came and we stood arm in arm, encircling what we had built, and did not move. These are our homes, we said, and the government scratched its head. It had never seen houses like ours—our constructions of wire and aluminum, of quilts and driftwood, of plastic tarps and rubber tires. The government came down from its machines to inspect these works of art. We showed them the places we had made, and eventually the government, not knowing what to do, left us alone.

You can have this land, it said. We don't want it anyway.

The newspapers wondered where the thousands had come from. How we had done it. And the radio asked as well, and the television sent cameras, and little by little we told some of our story. The nights spent in the endless city, collecting the materials that would become

our homes. The mornings sorting through it, puzzling together homes out of these odds and ends. We saved some of the story for ourselves, like the words of the songs we sang, and the contents of our prayers.

One day, the government decided to count us, but it didn't take long before someone decided the task was impossible, and so new maps were drawn, and on the empty space that had existed on the northeastern edge of the city the cartographers now wrote *The Thousands*. And we liked the name because numbers were all we'd ever had.

Of course, we are many more than that now.

Daniel Alarcón is an associate editor of the magazine *Etiqueta Negra*. His novel, *Lost City Radio*, was published in 2007.